Fade Out

"It's simple," thought Jake, "I hate myself. I'm sick of being Jake Stone. I've tried to change and I can't. I don't like the way I look. I don't like the way I act. I don't like the way I dress. I don't even like the sound of my voice. I want to fade out of the picture and let someone else be Jake. I've been Jake long enough. Let someone else take a turn."

**Other Apple Paperbacks
you will enjoy:**

The Trouble with Jake's Double

Dean Marney

AN
APPLE
PAPERBACK

SCHOLASTIC INC.
New York Toronto London Auckland Sydney

For Luke,
who very much likes being Luke.

ISBN 0-590-40557-8

12 11 10 9 8 7 6 5 4 3 2 1   8 9/8 0 1 2 3/9

Printed in the U.S.A.   01

First Scholastic printing, January 1988

Chapter 1

Jake Stone was lying on his bed eating popcorn and reading a new book he'd just checked out of the library. He was reading slowly. He wasn't usually a fast reader, but this time he wanted to make sure that he didn't miss a word of this book. The book's title was *Change Your Mind and You Can Change Your World*. Jake's world could use some changing.

Jake thought he was a nerd, plain and simple. He was sure everyone else thought so, too. He actually had some pretty good evidence to prove it.

Everyone picked on him, and when they weren't picking on him he picked on himself. He picked his nose till his mother would scream, "It's going to bleed!" or until his dad would yell at him and tell him to watch out or, "You'll pull your brains out."

Jake also picked at his scabs. He had quite

a few. He was sort of the type that fell down a lot. A few of the kids called him "the mop" because once while playing basketball in PE, he kept getting tied up in his own feet and falling down, so finally the instructor said, "We've got a janitor to clean the floors, Stone! What do you think you are? A mop?"

Jake didn't think he had too many friends. He figured that everyone thought he was too sickening. He was the only kid to throw up in the first grade. He was the only kid to wet his pants in the third grade.

Jake once thought he was in love. It was in the fifth grade. He wrote Jennifer Lake a note saying:

> *Jennifer, I think you are beautiful.*
> *Love,*
> *Jake*

When Jennifer read the note she screamed like someone had stabbed her. She stood up right during school and said, "Jake, if you ever do that again I'm going to have you locked up."

Her dad was a policeman. Jake didn't think he should take any chances. He didn't even give her a Valentine during the Valentine's Day exchange for fear she might really do it.

Jake tried to not let it bother him when people said things to him. He pretended that he didn't hear them. Of course he did, and it always made his stomach sting and his neck stiff to have someone call him creepy or worse.

It wasn't like Jake didn't try to be better, but no matter what he did, things just didn't work out. He'd be all dressed for school in what he thought were perfect clothes and someone would say, "Hey, Jake, do you have another pair of shoes like that at home?" He would look down and see that he had put on two different shoes.

No one else noticed if other people's pants were a little too short but if Jake's were, they said, "Hey, Jake, where's the flood?"

Jake felt like he couldn't put it all together. Even if he wore the best clothes he had, combed his hair, and had a clean handkerchief, something would happen to ruin it. It could be that he slipped on something or tripped over a rock and put a large hole in his pants.

Certainly if he didn't fall down he would step in dog doo. If there was any within a five-mile radius, his feet found it. He would scrape it off, rub his shoes in dirt and then slide them across a mile of grass and still someone would say, "Mrs. Archer, I think someone has stepped in something smelly, and it's making me sick to my stomach. May I be excused?" The whole class would turn and look at Jake. They knew it was him.

Bubble gum had a way of finding Jake, and of all places it usually found his hair. He gave up ever chewing it because it seemed that no matter how small a bubble he tried to blow, it would immediately get out of hand and pop in his hair. The only way to get it out was to cut it out. This gave Jake's hair a very unusual look.

Jake was in the sixth grade, and he was clear about one thing. He didn't want to be himself anymore. He never wanted to feel bad again.

When Jake saw the book *Change Your Mind and You Can Change Your World* on the shelf in the library, he knew it was what he needed. The cover of the book said, *"You can create anything with the power of your mind!"* Jake knew what he wanted to create.

Jake dreamed of having a double. He wished for someone else who looked like him. Someone he could send places and have him do the things that embarrassed Jake or made him feel bad. Jake could just stay away and avoid everything unpleasant.

No one would see Jake fall down or see his shoes didn't quite match. Nothing would happen to the real Jake. It would happen to someone who looked like him. It would be like the real Jake didn't exist.

He took another handful of popcorn and read:

Your mind creates what you experience. Change what you think and you change what you experience. Be careful! You always get what you want! Choose carefully what you want. Thoughts are real things.

Jake whistled a commercial he had heard on the radio and decided right then and there that he wanted to create a double. "I'm going to do it!" he said.

Chapter 2

It's simple," thought Jake. "I hate myself. I'm sick of being Jake Stone. I've tried to change and I can't. I don't like the way I look. I don't like the way I act. I don't like the way I dress. I don't even like the sound of my voice. I want to fade out of the picture and let someone else be Jake. I've been Jake long enough. Let someone else take a turn."

Jake had it all figured out. It made total sense to him. With what he could learn from the book he would create his double.

He was so excited about what he was going to do that he just had to tell someone. The book said not to run out and tell everyone what you really want because they'll just tell you why you can't have it or they will laugh at you. Jake was sure that Margery would never laugh at his brilliant plan.

Margery was a year older than Jake. She was probably the only person who Jake felt truly liked him. Jake suspected that Margery liked him because she was the only person who had more problems than Jake. This was partially true, but Margery also had grown up two doors down the street from Jake and had always liked him.

Margery's biggest problem was her dirty, greasy hair. She told everyone that she liked it that way. The truth was that Margery was afraid of getting her head wet. She once told Jake that she was sure she was going to drown if she got her head wet.

"I must have drowned in some past life. You know, like I think I was probably a pirate who had to walk the plank."

Jake figured that anyone who thought she had a past life as a pirate wouldn't laugh when he said he was going to create his double.

Jake told Margery.

Margery said, "You are what?"

Jake repeated, "I'm going to create my double."

Jake had been wrong; the book had been right. She laughed her head off.

She said, "That could be the craziest thing I've ever heard of. Who do you think you are, Dr. Frankenstein?"

"You don't understand," said Jake.

"Of course I don't understand. How do you understand that?"

Jake looked hurt

"Jake, you have to admit it's pretty weird." Margery tried to stop laughing.

Jake still looked hurt.

"Okay," said Margery. "Never kill a good idea till you've tested it. How are you going to do it? Do we have to dig up any dead bodies? You know I won't touch anything dead." Margery couldn't stand to even clean up dead flies. "Death goes against my nature," she always said.

"Dang!" said Margery, jumping ahead. "I just got this flash of Margery and Jake Robots, Inc., and I kind of like the ring of it."

"It isn't going to be a robot."

"Okay, so we'll call it Jake and Margery Robots, Inc. I have to say you drive a hard bargain."

"I'm not making a robot!" screamed Jake.

"Well, what is this double going to be?" asked Margery.

"It's going to be something I create with the powers of my mind."

"Are you serious?" asked Margery. "Because if you are, people may try to put you away in an institution or something."

Jake walked over and climbed the nearest tree. When life was at its worst Jake felt better up in a tree. He also did it because Margery hated heights. She never followed him up. This time she followed him up anyway. Jake looked at her, his mouth wide open.

"Don't look so surprised. I don't have to be afraid of everything, do I?" Margery gulped. "I'm telling you, if they have to call the fire department to get me down it is going to be your fault, and you'll have to pay the bill."

"There is no bill."

"There is, too," said Margery.

"The bill is to the city. The fire department is tax supported."

Margery thought for a minute. "Who cares?"

They were now both sitting on the same limb. Margery looked only straight ahead.

"If I look down I'll probably throw up or even worse, I'll faint. That means I'll fall and probably break my neck and die. You know how I feel about death. Why are you doing this to me? Why did you make me come up here?"

Jake didn't say a word.

Margery said, "So why don't you pick flying?"

"I wish you would take me seriously," said Jake.

Margery laughed. "But how can I? You've told me you're going to create yourself into two people just by using your mind. Is this some kind of weird fantasy?"

"I have a book," said Jake. "It explains everything."

"Where is it?" asked Margery with just a touch of enthusiasm.

Jake smiled. "I knew you'd understand. I knew you'd help."

Margery said, "I did not say I'd help! Two of you I couldn't stand."

Jake said, "Some friend," and started down the tree.

"Okay," she said, "I love blackmail. I'll help, but you have to get me down from here and fast, and you have to go get a ladder and a safety rope."

Jake scrambled down the tree and ran to his garage.

"Hurry," yelled Margery, "I feel faint."

Chapter 3

Accoording to the book it is very easy to get what you want," said Jake.

"Uh-huh," said Margery, trying to keep a straight face.

"All you have to do is know exactly what you want and then concentrate on it."

"Simple," said Margery, raising her eyebrows.

"You are treating me like a second-grader."

"I'm so sorry," said Margery.

"The key is to think about what you want so much that you believe it is real and then — "

"Hocus-pocus we have another Jake?"

"Something like that," said Jake.

"Where did you get all this? I thought you'd only read chapter one."

"I did. It was all in chapter one."

"I can't imagine what would be in chapter two."

"I'm not really sure I need to read more," said Jake.

"You could be making a mistake," said Margery.

Margery and Jake were sitting on the Stones' back porch. Margery was trying to juggle two tennis balls. Jake had told her it wasn't juggling unless you used at least three balls. Margery had told him to mind his own business and "for your information I'm working up to three balls."

Jake was holding his book like his fingers were attached to it.

"Let me think this through for a minute," said Margery. Margery always liked to think things through. "You mean," she said, "that I could have clean hair just by thinking about it?"

"Well . . ." said Jake. He didn't like to think things through.

"That's what you said."

"I think you should try something bigger," said Jake.

"That is not what you said," Margery fired back.

"Okay," said Jake, "you can think clean hair if you want to. It just seems kind of small."

"Small to you. Perhaps you'd like being a human french fry," Margery said. "All right. This is okay. You think yourself into doubles or whatever you are going to call it, and I'll think myself into clean hair."

"It's a deal," said Jake. "You need someone to keep you going. I think we should start right now. What do you think?"

Suddenly Margery didn't like this whole thing at all. "It's so stupid," she said to herself, but she didn't want to be another person who made fun of Jake. He may not have been the greatest, but he was her friend. Margery thought, "We're even blood brother and sister, from that time Jake made us pick our knee scabs and then rub the sores together. Yuck!" She also figured that he'd get tired of the whole thing and forget about it by tomorrow.

"Okay," said Margery, "let's get this over with."

They both crossed their legs and started thinking. Jake thought about his double. Margery thought about clean hair.

After ten minutes Margery batted her eyelashes and said, "How do I look?"

Chapter 4

You simply can't believe everything you read," said Margery as she sat down in front of her mirror. She had a desk in her room with a mirror above it. She used it to practice making monster faces or to remind herself that she was ugly and had dirty hair. Walking by the mirror she never failed to pause and say, "Hi, ugly. Nice hair."

This time she looked in the mirror and said, "I'm beautiful and I now have clean hair." She then added, "I now have clean, beautiful, shiny hair." She closed her eyes.

She tried to think of how she would look with clean hair all the time. "Unusual," she answered herself. She could just barely remember how she looked when her mother would absolutely make her wash her hair. She thought of how she liked the feel of clean hair and even if she acted otherwise she even liked it when her mother told her how nice it looked. "Maybe I don't have such bad hair," she thought.

She opened her eyes. "Nothing," she said. "Greasy as ever. How can it work? The only way to get clean hair is to wash it."

She went downstairs. Suddenly she was overcome with desire for a glass of water. It was like she was in the desert. She had to have water.

She ran to the faucet and drank three glasses. When she finished, she freaked. "I'm going crazy!" she screamed.

Her father from the living room said, "What else is new?"

"I am," she yelled. "I hate water and I just drank an entire glass."

"How was it?"

"Wonderful," she said weakly.

Margery didn't know quite what to do. She hadn't drunk water — just plain water — for almost a year. She had said it was part of her fear of drowning. When her parents noticed she'd stopped drinking water they talked about it forever and then decided she'd grow out of it, and in the meantime it was nice she drank so much milk because it made strong bones and teeth. Margery did drink tons of milk. To her knowledge no one had ever drowned in milk.

Margery then had an urge to take a bath. It was only the slightest urge, but it was still an urge. A bath to Margery was usually two inches of water and two feet of bubbles so you couldn't tell how deep it really was. That was in case her mother should come barging into the bathroom. Margery hated it when her mother did that, and she told her mother to please stop. Her mother told her that if she didn't want company she should lock the door. Margery felt she should keep the door unlocked in case someone should have to come in quickly and save her from drowning. "Only come in if I'm drowning," said Margery.

"Really, Margery," said her mother, "don't be morbid."

"I can't believe I wanted to take a bath. This is too weird," she said.

Over at Jake's house, if you listened carefully you might have been able to hear Jake up in his room chanting. Over and over he was saying, "I have someone else to take my place. I have a twin. I have someone who does everything for me." He kept saying it over and over.

His mother came by his room, stuck her head in, and said, "Are you singing, Jake? How nice," and then left. Jake went on chanting.

As far as Jake was concerned nothing was happening. He did feel his skin tingle a little, but he thought that was caused by breathing too fast and too much while he repeated and repeated his thoughts out loud.

"Well," he said, "I didn't expect it to happen today."

Chapter 5

The alarm clock went off in Jake's room. It wasn't Jake's alarm; it was his older brother Sam's. Sam was in high school and got up early to go to swimming practice.

Since he could remember, Jake had always slept in the same room with his brother Sam unless they had company. Then either one or both of them would end up sleeping in the basement. He didn't mind sharing the room. He liked Sam a lot. He never let Sam know it but he did.

Jake would have gone anywhere with Sam or done anything with him. Sam was nice about it, but he didn't exactly feel the same way about Jake. It wasn't that he hadn't tried.

Sam took Jake swimming with him once. Sam did a beautiful double back flip off the high dive. Jake followed him, planning on doing just a plain dive.

He hit the water, losing his swimming suit, and then hit the bottom of the pool with his face, and gave himself a bloody nose. Everyone said to Sam, "I can't believe he is your brother."

Sam played catch with Jake twice in his life. Jake broke a window each time attempting a curve ball.

When Jake was much younger, Sam tried taking him to the movies. The picture was *Snow White* and Jake got so scared of the wicked stepmother he started to bawl and had to be taken home.

Sam wasn't scared of anything. He was excellent at every sport he played, and he played them all. He looked good, was popular, and hardly ever got into trouble. Jake felt it was unfair he had such a perfect older brother. It made him look even worse.

Sam was also super smart. It seemed to Jake that he never had to study. The truth was Sam liked to get his work done at school. If he did have homework he did it right after dinner. Then he was gone. He had a girlfriend named Joan.

Jake liked Joan, too. He thought she was pretty. He never said so, though. He said dumb things like, "Sam are you going to go see phony Joanie who is very boney and has the breath of a pony?"

Sam would call Jake a "stupid creep," tackle him, sit on him, and tie his shoelaces together in knots. "That'll teach you, you little nerd," he'd say.

Jake, for the record, also had an older sister, Maria. Maria was fifteen, and most of the time she pretended that Jake didn't exist. Jake preferred it that way.

Every once in a while she would notice him and say, "Mom, has Jake changed his socks lately?" or "Mom, Jake is wearing that shirt outside again."

Jake had a shirt printed with the saying, ROCK AND ROLL UNTIL YOU VOMIT. He loved it. He bought it with his own money. His mother hated it. "What will people think I'm raising? Some kind of sick juvenile criminal. If I catch you even looking outside with it on, I'll burn it. That shirt does not leave this house!"

Jake waited until Sam had gotten up, packed his gym bag, and gone downstairs before he sat up. He then crossed his legs in what he thought sort of looked like a yoga position and started chanting.

"There are two of me. I no longer have to feel or do anything. My double does it all for me."

When he got up and looked in the mirror he almost screamed. But the scream got caught first in his throat, then his nose. He sounded like an elephant with a cold. Jake looked blurry. Then a very faint gray shadow appeared around his edges. Then with a huge tug it pulled itself away from Jake and walked out the door.

"Is it the light?" he thought. "Maybe it was sitting in that position too long. Sitting like that must do something to your brain." At breakfast his mother said, "Jake, are you feeling well? Are you getting sick?"

Jake said, "No."

"Well, something is different about you," his mother said.

He practically ran to school. He saw Margery across the street, and forgetting where he was yelled, "I think something happened. I'm not sure though. I think I split in half this morning."

Someone behind Margery who heard him yelled back, "You've split all right. Split in the head."

Chapter 6

Margery had borrowed the book from Jake. "I need it for a while," she had said. "You aren't reading it anyway." Jake had to admit that she was telling the truth. Jake had never been too much for finishing books.

Jake said, "I go for the good parts. You should try it."

Margery opened the book, thumbed through it, and read where her eyes landed. *The whole secret to getting what you want is knowing exactly what you want.*

"That is certainly basic," said Margery. She was on her bed preparing to paint her toenails. She was trying not to spill nail polish on her white bedspread. She was also trying to paint her toenails without her glasses because she forgot where she took them off.

In order to see both her toenails and the book, she had the book propped next to her on a tower of stuffed animals and pillows. She had her knees drawn up almost to her chin so she looked like she was doing a full cannon into a swimming pool.

The whole secret to getting what you want is knowing exactly what you want. Realizing she had read that line before she said, "I heard you the first time and besides any second-grader could figure that one out." She read on.

> *You may think this is extremely basic and something a second-grader should know. . . .*

"Certainly do," commented Margery.

> *However, the truth is, very few people know what they want. They say, 'Oh, I want to be rich' or 'I want to be beautiful' but what does that mean? Do they want $100 or $1,000,000? Do they want brown hair or blonde?*

Margery said, "A million dollars will be just fine for me, thank you."

> *Knowing exactly what you want, if I may be permitted to repeat myself, is the key that unlocks the door to getting what you want. Now what do you really want?*

"You want to know what I want?" said Margery. "I'll tell you. I want clean hair, and I want it without getting wet."

She returned to the book.

Now if you know what you want, say it out loud. Say to the universe, "I want this. How do I get it?" The universe will never fail to provide.

"Okay, universe," said Margery, "I want clean hair, and I want it without getting wet."

She sat for a moment and waited for something to happen. Realizing she had forgotten something she quickly added, "Tell me how to get it."

She waited some more. Nothing happened. She finished painting her toenails. Still nothing happened. She found some nail polish remover and tried to take the spot off her bedspread where she had spilled just a little.

She looked in her mirror. "Maybe it takes a while," she thought. "I probably should get something to eat while I'm waiting."

She went downstairs, opened the refrigerator door, and took inventory. Two apples, some cheese, and not much else was in sight.

"I hope Mom went shopping." She grabbed one of the apples and the cheese. As she was cutting a piece of cheese her mother walked in the door.

"How did you find anything to eat in that refrigerator?"

"It wasn't easy," said Margery.

"I went shopping, and you wouldn't believe the crowd. I waited in line for a cart. Can you imagine waiting in line for a grocery cart? First of the month is always that way. I should know better."

She started unpacking a grocery sack. "Margery, be a sweetheart and go out to the car and haul in some sacks, would you?"

Margery said, "Okay. I don't have anything else to do."

On top of the first bag she brought in was a can of something called DRY AS A BONE, a dry shampoo. She read the label. *Shake and spray. Wait five minutes and then brush out. You now have squeaky clean hair without getting wet.*

Her mother saw her looking at the can. "Yes," she said with some irritation in her voice, "I bought that for you, but it doesn't mean you use it all the time. Notice it says for in between washings. I don't know why such a beautiful girl as yourself refuses to keep her hair clean."

"I hate water," said Margery. She was feeling scared — like things were out of control. She had asked for clean hair without getting wet and she had received it.

"Of course you don't," said her mother. "I

like water. Your father likes water. You like water."

Margery was pretty much in a state of shock. She went back out to the car to get another sack. As she got outside she looked up toward the sky and said, "Well, thank you universe."

She didn't know her dad was coming around the corner of the house. "What did you say?"

"Oh, nothing. It is just an experiment," said Margery.

"Science?" he asked.

"Ya," said Margery, "I guess."

Chapter 7

Jake ran to catch up with Margery. "It's not working," he said, out of breath, "Nothing is happening. I'll need the book back."

"You can't have it," Margery said.

"What do you mean?"

"I mean you can't have it. I'm not done with it yet," said Margery.

"You have to share. I'm the one that checked it out," said Jake, still trying to catch his breath.

"I returned it to the library this morning and rechecked it out in my name," said Margery, looking Jake straight in the eye.

Jake was almost starting to cry. "You're lying. I have to have it back."

Margery said, "Well, I'm starting to get results and I want to keep going and I'm not lying. I can't risk having you lose it."

"So do what you're doing. You don't need the book to do that." Jake grabbed the book off the top of Margery's book bag.

"Stop it, you idiot!" she screamed. Jake started to run.

Margery dropped the rest of her stuff and took off after him. She managed to just grab ahold of the back of his shirt and then slipped her hand down an inch so she was hanging on to his belt.

"Stop," she panted.

Jake kept running, pulling her along. They looked like two little kids playing horse. Margery, getting tired, gave a wild jerk on Jake's belt and at the same time threw her weight to the right, dumping them both into Mrs. McCafery's front yard shrubs.

"She's going to kill us," said Margery.

She was right. Mrs. McCafery came bounding out her front door, both arms beating at something imaginary in the air, with two dogs first behind her and then out in front of her, barking and looking very much like police dogs after criminals.

"We're dead," said Jake.

"Don't just sit there. Run," said Margery.

"We're sorry," yelled Jake, now standing but not running.

"No, you're not," yelled Mrs. McCafery without slowing down.

"You're right," Jake said to Margery, "run." Then to Mrs. McCafery, "Yes we are."

They ran nonstop for blocks until Margery said, "I'm going to puke. I mean it."

They were clear over on the other side of

town from their houses and were faced with a long trip back — first, to where Margery threw her stuff down, and then home, going completely around Mrs. McCafery's house.

"That was really dumb," said Jake. "Why did you pick her shrubs to tackle me into?"

"I didn't tackle you. I pulled you over and it seems to me that you were running away with my book."

Jake still had the book under his arm. "I had it first," he said.

Margery said, "It was going to be overdue. I just took care of it for you. You should be grateful."

Jake was stumped. He knew she was telling the truth, sort of.

"I've got a side ache. Do you suppose I'm having an appendicitis attack?" asked Margery.

"No, you are not," said Jake with some disgust. "Pant. That's what my brother told me to do when I had a side ache. Pant."

"Like a dog?"

"Exactly," said Jake. He knew she would do it, too. If he had told her that his brother had said to take off your shoes and suck your toes two at a time she would have done it. It was no secret to anyone (though Margery thought it was) that Margery was madly in love with Sam.

Margery panted so fast she hyperventilated and had to lie down. After what seemed like hours she said she felt better. They started walking. Jake still had the book.

"Just let me look something up in chapter fourteen," said Margery.

"I'd be happy to look it up for you," said Jake.

"Oh, Jake, please," she pleaded. "Let's cooperate on this."

"You sound like *Sesame Street*."

She stuck her tongue out at him.

"Okay," he said, "but we have to share."

"All right," she said. "I'll take it one night and then you can have it the next."

"That's fair," said Jake. "Who gets it tonight?"

"I think I should," said Margery.

"I think I should because I'm going to be grounded tonight in my room because you pushed me into Mrs. McCafery's yard, and she'll for sure call my mom."

"She couldn't have seen who you were."

"We'll see."

Mrs. McCafery went to Jake's church and knew all his family. She was quite famous for calling parents to report that their brats had stepped on her lawn.

"She has a right to keep kids from ruining her yard," Jake's mother had said.

"But she is so nuts about it," Jake had said.

"Just stay away from her yard," were the last instructions Jake's mother gave him on the subject.

"Okay, you can have the book, but I get it tomorrow, bright and early," said Margery. "Do you mind if I look at it for just a minute?"

Margery stopped, opened the book, and read out loud.

Affirm, affirm, and affirm again. Say positive things, write positive things, think positive things. What you desire is coming to you now. Picture it clearly.

Margery then added, "You cannot believe what I have pictured."

Jake said, "Right." He was picturing something far different from clean hair. He was picturing something far more dangerous and it *was* coming to him now. He was picturing another Jake Stone. He was picturing two Jakes. Jake thought, "He can get in trouble for falling in Mrs. McCafery's bushes." A perfect Jake to take his place.

Chapter 8

Jake's mother answered the phone. "Hello," she said. The line was incredibly crackly and she could barely hear.

"Hello," said a voice on the other end.

"Yes?" said Jake's mother. "I can't hear you. You'll have to speak up."

"I'm sort of weak," said the voice.

"I really can't hear you. What leak?"

"Norma?" said the voice.

"Yes, it's me."

"I'm your cousin Nathan."

She heard that clearly but for the life of her couldn't think of a cousin Nathan. "Excuse me," she said, "but I don't remember a cousin Nathan. How close of cousins are we?"

The voice grew faint again. "Closer than you think," it said.

"Pardon me, but I don't understand what pink has to do with being cousins," said Jake's mother.

"I'm your uncle" — the voice was interrupted by a crackle — "son."

"Would that be Uncle Ned's son? Well, it would have to be. He's the only one that had children, but goodness, I hardly knew him. You know the family lost track. He was sort of the black sheep of the family. Well, I shouldn't be telling you that."

The voice continued, "Anyway, I'm going to be in town, and I'd like to come see you. Maybe stay awhile if it is all right?"

Jake's mother said, "Well of course, family is family. Should we pick you up at the airport?"

"No, I'll just show up at your front door."

Jake's mother said, "Now when can I expect you?"

The voice was very weak. "I don't know," it crackled. "I can't tell."

"Who fell?" said Jake's mother.

"I'll probably be there tomorrow."

"How nice. Now it's Nathan, isn't it?"

"Yes, see you tomorrow."

Jake's mother set down the receiver. "Oh my," she said. "This place is a pit and my cousin Nathan, my long lost cousin — let me see, that makes him the kids' first cousin once removed — will be here tomorrow. Oh my, where are we going to put him?"

"Who?" said Jake's dad.

"My cousin Nathan," she answered.

"You never told me about a cousin Nathan," said Jake's dad.

"That is because I never knew about him till now," said Jake's mother.

"Norma, you know how I feel about the odd members of your family and their extended stays."

"I think he is only staying for a night . . . maybe two."

"See what I mean?" said Jake's dad. "Give them an inch and they take a mile."

"Now Norman, try to be nice. Family is family. Jake," called his mother, "Sam, Maria, come here.

"I have some tremendous news for you," Jake's mother said. Jake didn't think she sounded quite like it was tremendous good news for him.

"What's wrong? Did Mrs. McCafery call you? I didn't mean to fall in her bushes. Honest."

"Jake!" His mother looked irritated and then said, "Well, I guess we need to talk about that later. But right now I want to tell you that my cousin Nathan is coming to visit us."

"What do you mean?" said Maria. "Who is cousin Nathan?"

"Jake, is there something wrong with you?" asked his mother before she continued. "You look different. Maybe you need a physical. You haven't been yourself lately."

"I'm fine," said Jake. "Really, I'm fine. Who's cousin Nathan?"

"How old is he?" asked Maria.

"Well, now, he's probably my age. I assumed he was my age. I probably should have asked. Goodness, I really don't know a thing about him. He could be from another planet for all I know. Well family is family, I always say, and won't it be nice to have a house guest."

"Move in, more like it," said Jake's father.

"To think I didn't even know I had a cousin Nathan. Isn't the world full of surprises?"

Jake felt a vibration in his brain.

"What's the matter, Jake? You look positively ill," said his mother.

"Nothing," said Jake. "I'm fine now. My head just felt weird for a second."

"Well, if you feel fine . . . I'd like you to run your little legs up to your room and clean it. I mean really clean it. Do not just pick it up. Do not just push everything into your closet. Clean it. That means dust, vacuum, the works. Sam could probably use some help moving his stuff to the basement also."

"I assume I'm in the basement?" said Sam.

"Correct," said his mother.

"I take it the company is sleeping with me in Sam's and my room," said Jake.

"You've got it."

"I don't feel *that* good," said Jake.

"Get to work," said his mother.

Jake went upstairs. Sam was already busy packing up his weights.

"Hey, squirt," Sam said, "would you help me carry these weights down to the basement?"

"Forget it," said Jake, "I'm supposed to clean up your mess."

"You know, squirt, I'm going to miss the way you always lend a helping hand."

Jake felt bad. He wished he'd said he would help Sam. "Here I go again," he thought. "I wish my double was here. He could carry the weights downstairs and clean up the room."

Jake started picking up. As he moved through the room he said over and over, "I can create my double." However, he doubted it was working.

"I know I can't create my double. Why am I pretending?" he said to his hocky puck, which he found in his underwear drawer. "So what. I'm a zero. I know it. Nobody likes me. That's just the way life is. I hate myself. Nathan won't be able to stand me either. Everyone in this family hates me. Sam hates me. Maria hates me. So what?"

Jake then sat down on a pile of clothes and started reading a comic book. He was sitting on top of his favorite pair of socks. He'd just found them underneath his bed. Although they were slightly stiff and unuseable in their present condition, he decided to celebrate their return by resting. He was just getting into it when his mother walked in the door.

"Nice try, Jake," she said. "Now try this one. No TV for a week."

"I was just resting," said Jake.

"I noticed," said his mother. "How would you like to try for two weeks?"

"I'm too tired. I need to rest," said Jake.

"Don't you think I'd like to rest? Don't you think I'd like to sit down and read a comic book? I work all day and then have to come home and do the housework. Jake, I need help. It would take three of me to get it all done properly. Now move."

She left and Jake tore into his room. He decided he was going to make himself make it sparkle. "After I create my double I'll teach my mother how to make three of herself."

Chapter 9

Are you feeling okay?" asked Margery. "You look funny."

"Oh, I just feel kind of depressed," said Jake.

"Cheer up," said Margery. "How's the project coming?"

"I've given up," said Jake to Margery. "How about you?"

"No, not yet. Aren't you getting any results?"

"Nothing," said Jake.

"Are you sure?"

"I'm positive. How about you?" asked Jake.

"Well, kind of," said Margery. "I mean, I've had some things happen that could be, you know, coincidence, but I don't know. Except, I woke up this morning thinking about signing up for swimming lessons, and I almost took a shower the other night."

"You've signed up for swimming lessons before," said Jake.

"My parents have signed me up," answered Margery.

"I don't think it means anything," said Jake.

Margery shrugged her shoulders. "Maybe not."

"Besides," said Jake, "I thought you weren't trying to get rid of your fear of water. I thought you were just trying to have clean hair."

"Well if you had read the book," said Margery, "he tells you that being afraid keeps you from getting what you really want. He suggests that you try to find anything you can to like about something you're afraid of even if it is just liking yourself for being afraid of the thing. Also he says be grateful for your fears and it changes them like magic. So I've been thinking about what I like about water and about being grateful for it."

"That's it?" said Jake.

"Well, I write 'I like water and water likes me.' "

"Like sentences a teacher makes you write when you are in trouble?" asked Jake.

"Not really," said Margery. "Honest, it's kind of fun."

Margery then took the book out of her pack and handed it to Jake.

"It's your turn," she said.

"You keep it. I've given up."

"Are you sure?" said Margery.

"Positive," said Jake, managing to let go of a huge sneeze that left wet spots on his sweatshirt.

"I think I'm going to be sick," said Margery.

"Got a Kleenex?" said Jake.

"Not on me," said Margery.

Jake took off his shirt and used it for a handkerchief. He then rolled it in a ball and put it under his arm.

"Good thing it's warm out," said Margery. Jake sniffed.

"Well," said Margery, "are you sure you don't want the book? I think you should keep trying. The book says you can have anything you want if you're willing to really want it. You sounded like you really wanted to create your double. But what do I know?"

"I don't know, either," said Jake. "I'll think about it."

"I'm also trying to spend some time picturing myself with clean hair. That's the hardest."

Jake finally laughed. "No kidding. I could never imagine you with clean hair."

"Stick it," said Margery.

Chapter 10

I can create my double.

  I can create my double.

  I can create my double.

  I can create my double.

  I can create my double.

Jake wrote the sentence a hundred times, mumbling it every time he wrote it. He heard the doorbell ring. He got up and looked out his window. He could just see through the branches of the tree in front of his window. There was a boy in front of the door.

He ran his fingers through his hair and went downstairs. The front door was open and his mother was standing on the porch.

"Hello," said Jake's mother. "Can I help you?"

"Yes, I hope so," said a nicely dressed young man about Jake's age. "Is this the Stone residence?"

"Why yes it is, and you must be here to see Jake." Jake had just joined his mother at the

door. "Jake, there is someone here to see you."
She then turned to the young man. "I'm sorry
but you can't stay long. You see we're expecting a guest. A cousin I didn't even know
I had is coming for a visit."

"Norma?" said the young man.

"Yes?" said Jake's mother.

"I'm your cousin Nathan."

"Of course you are dear." Then what
Nathan had said registered. "I mean, of course
you're not. Oh, my. You're much too young. I
mean. Well, I was expecting someone older.
You're closer to Jake's age than mine.

"I would guess," said Nathan, "we're closer
in age than anyone thinks. I mean, my mother
and dad had me late in life."

Jake's mother stood there looking at
Nathan. "I don't know what has come over
me. Where are my manners? I just expected
someone older, you understand, and now I
can't get over how much you look like Jake."

It was true. He did look an awful lot like
Jake. But if they had looked closely they
would have noticed a few differences.

Jake's mother rubbed her eyes. "I seem to
be falling apart before your eyes, Nathan. I
have to go sit down. You look blurry to me
and I seem to be so dizzy."

"I'm sure you'll be fine in a minute," said
Nathan. "How do you do, Jake?" Nathan extended his hand.

After a second Jake took it. Immediately

he felt his knees go weak. He thought, "He's pulling me apart." Jake felt something leave his body.

Nathan said, "Now that wasn't so bad, was it?"

"What?" said Jake, shaking his head.

"I'll do everything," said Nathan.

Jake's mother felt better in a minute. "For a minute I felt like I was being hypnotized or something. Like I was losing consciousness for a second."

"I'm glad you're feeling better now, Mrs. Stone."

"Oh, Nathan, call me Norma."

"Thank you, Norma. It feels really great to be here."

"How was your trip. Smooth?" asked Jake's mother.

"Very," said Nathan.

"Did you fly?" asked Jake.

"Oh, you could say that," said Nathan.

"I think I'm feeling dizzy again," said Jake's mother. "I think I'd better go upstairs and lie down for a minute. Can you two fend for yourselves until dinner?"

"Of course," said Nathan.

"Ya, of course," said Jake.

"Well, isn't it nice I already decided that you would stay in Jake's room with him, since you're both so close in age. How nicely it will all work out."

"Of course," said Nathan.

Jake's mother headed upstairs to her bedroom. Jake showed Nathan the way to their room.

"How long are you staying?" asked Jake.

Jake thought he heard Nathan say, "As long as you desire." But he convinced himself that he must have really heard two weeks.

Chapter 11

Margery just couldn't believe that creating "things" could be this easy. She was thinking that if it was this simple then everyone should be doing it. She was thinking all this as she thumbed through the book at the kitchen table.

Under her feet was her cat Dinah. Margery had her shoes and socks off and was petting the cat with her bare foot. The cat purred complete approval.

She read the start of chapter eight:

> *If you start to get results and it scares you, relax. You're normal. Most people read something about how you can create what you want with your mind and they think it can't be that easy. They think, 'Why, if you could just get anything by thinking about it, isn't everyone a millionaire?'*

I'll be honest with you. They aren't millionaires because they aren't thinking about being millionaires.

Some people say, "Well, I know for a fact that it just doesn't work."

But it does work. It works all the time. However, it usually works in the reverse, the negative. People think worried thoughts about not having enough money and that is what they get, not enough money. They think about being old, sick, and dying and that's what they get.

Margery's mother walked into the room. "What are you reading?"

"Oh, this mind book."

Her mother looked a bit surprised. "What's it about?" she asked.

"You know, it's just about how you use your mind and stuff."

"Oh, I see," said her mother. "Could I read it when you're done?"

Margery's mother had this big thing about reading what Margery read. She thought it made her a better parent. It just irritated Margery.

"Well," said Margery, "I've kind of promised it to someone else."

Margery felt that books were personal. You can tell things about people by the books they read. Margery felt special when she gave someone a book she really liked to read.

Margery didn't want her mother to read this book. If her mother kept bugging her about it she would just tell her that she had to take it back to the library because it was over-due. That was her standard response when she had a book that she didn't want her mother to read.

Margery couldn't help but think, "What would my mother think of me for reading this book?" She was slightly embarrassed. She didn't feel comfortable having her mother know everything about her.

Margery moved to the living room and reread the passage in the book about writing goals down and being very specific. She wrote down her goal.

It had changed from her original one of having clean hair. The book said it was okay to change your goals. Goals should change as you get more information.

"My goal is to love water," she wrote.

She thought that would cover it. If she loved water she'd love washing in it, drinking it, swimming in it. Her problems would be gone.

The book said she should write her goal down daily and think about it. She was doing that. It also said to measure your progress, but sometimes you had to look hard for ways to measure that progress. Sometimes the changes that go on are very subtle, and although those changes are very subtle they are there.

She had to look *subtle* up in the dictionary. She found it meant something difficult to understand or distinguish. Margery then had one of her urges for water.

She wasn't just thirsty. She couldn't have had juice or something. Instead, she had to have a glass of water.

Margery also had the urge to tell Jake. She grabbed the phone off the hook and called him.

"It happened again," she said.

"You've got to come over and meet my first cousin once removed," he paused and added "sometime."

"What do you mean sometime?"

"Well, I don't mean right now. That's what I mean."

"Fine," answered Margery.

"Now why did you call?" asked Jake.

"I forgot," said Margery.

"Everyone here says my cousin looks just like me but only better."

"Oh, really. Could you speak up? You're kind of hard to hear."

"Well, I've got to go now."

"Ya, sure. See you later."

Margery hung up. "Sorry I called."

She went upstairs and wrote a list of ten good things about water.

1. It's pretty (if you like water).
2. It's nice for fish.
3. It makes plants green when they're dying. Especially because my mother always forgets to water the plants.
4. It's nice for ducks to float on.
5. It gets things clean.
6. It sounds good if it's moving. Like when it's a creek or a river or the ocean.
7. It cools you off when you're hot.
8. It mixes well with Kool-Aid.
9. It drives certain people I don't care for crazy when it drips. Mrs. Thompson had a drippy faucet in her classroom all last year, and she said it drove her crazy. We all knew she didn't have far to go.
10. It cleans hair.

She thought, "Well, now I've said it. It cleans hair. I don't really think that is so wonderful, but some people might."

Chapter 12

Something weird was happening at Jake's house. He was getting ready to come down to dinner. Nathan had changed his clothes, but he still looked real neat and tidy. Jake had on a ripped up T-shirt. Nathan pulled a shirt out of his suitcase and said, "Why don't you try wearing this. It would look good on you."

Jake said, "Thanks," and not wanting to hurt Nathan's feelings, he put it on. He also went in the bathroom and brushed his hair. He left his fingernails dirty in case his mother wanted to know if it was really him.

His mother didn't actually say anything about how he looked at the table, but when he came into the room he did notice that her eyes opened a little wider than they had been used to opening.

Jake's dad made sure that Nathan monopolized the dinner conversation. He kept asking him questions. He asked him about everything — how old he was, where he was from. He practically asked his blood type.

A couple of times Jake tried to butt in and tell everyone something — anything — but no one could take their eyes off of Nathan.

"Don't interrupt," his father said.

Finally Jake's dad got the same look his mother had earlier when she first met Nathan. He said, "I'm feeling a little dizzy. You'll have to excuse me. I'm going to go lie down. I guess I asked too many questions."

Nathan said, "I seem to have that effect on people."

Through dinner Jake had tried to copy Nathan by putting his napkin on his lap. He also tried to sit completely in his chair instead of sitting with one foot on the ground ready to make a run for it. He even caught himself saying please and thank you. However, he didn't think his mother even noticed.

He was feeling a little funny in his gut. It was like a cross between car sickness and homesickness. He knew he wasn't carsick and he told himself he couldn't be homesick because he was at home. "You can't feel homesick at home," he told himself.

He felt lonely. "But how," he thought, "can you be lonely with people around you? I am so stupid. I really hate myself."

He sat through dessert wishing someone would talk to him. He wished that his dad would've been as interested in him sometime as he was in Nathan. Jake accidentally burped.

His mother turned to him and said, "Really, don't you have some homework?"

Jake started to answer, but before he could fully get his mouth to work Nathan was saying, "Could I help you with the dishes?"

Sam started laughing.

"What is so hysterical?" his mother asked Sam. She then turned to Nathan and said, "No Nathan, not tonight, but we'll be sure and take you up on it some other night."

Sam said to Nathan, "It is just that I don't think anyone has ever asked my mother that. It just struck me as funny."

"I thought I had said something wrong," said Nathan.

"Hardly," Jake's mother said.

"Well," said Sam, "maybe Nathan can help you with your homework, Jake. We all know you could certainly use some. Help, that is."

Jake cringed.

"I'd be glad to if I can," said Nathan.

They all got up from the dining room table. Nathan had grabbed their dirty plates and was carrying them into the kitchen and then headed for the stairs. Jake was last in line and was getting ready to slug Sam and say, "Got you last."

It was a game they played after dinner. The object was to not be the last one hit, so you would hit someone, yell "Got you last!" and run. Tonight Sam was too busy talking to Nathan because Nathan wanted Sam to work with him on his butterfly stroke. Sam had wanted to help Jake with his strokes a million times, but Jake wasn't interested.

"They're okay for me," he always said.

Jake said loudly to both Sam and Nathan, "Well, I'm going upstairs to do my homework."

Nathan said, "Great, I'll be right up. I just have to talk to Sam for a minute."

Jake went upstairs just as the phone rang.

Chapter 13

"Telephone for you, Jake," his mother said.

"Hi, Margery," said Jake. He knew it was Margery because she was the only person who ever called him, and he also knew she would be dying by now to hear about his cousin.

"Hi, yourself," said Margery. "What's going on over at your place?"

"We just ate dinner."

"How old is he?" asked Margery.

"Who?" Jake asked.

"You know exactly who."

"Oh, him," said Jake. "That who. He's my age."

"Is he cute?"

"My mother says he looks just like me."

"That bad?" said Margery.

"How's your hair?" said Jake.

"I'll ignore that snide remark," said Margery. "What's he doing right now?"

"Who?"

"Do we have to do this again? Your cousin."

"Why are you so interested?"

"I just am," said Margery. "What's his name?"

"His name is Nathan, and he's talking to Sam. Nope, he's not talking to Sam any longer. He's gone upstairs to help me with my homework."

"Math?"

"Ya, how did you know?"

"You could use some help."

"Did you call me just to check on my cousin?"

"Sort of, but also I wanted to tell you about this part in the book I just read."

"Could we talk about it later?" said Jake. "I have to do my homework. Nathan is waiting."

"It just said that you can create really bad things for yourself if you aren't careful and that you shouldn't panic if you do. If you remember to love yourself there are no mistakes that can't be corrected."

"To tell you the truth Margery, I'm not interested in the book anymore."

"Well, you asked me about my hair."

"I've really got to go," said Jake.

"Excuse me for living," said Margery.

"See you tomorrow," said Jake.

"Are you bringing him to school?"

"Ya," said Jake. "He said it would be fun to visit."

"Good," said Margery and she hung up.

"Good-bye," said Jake to a dead receiver. He then ran upstairs where Nathan was sitting at his desk working furiously at a piece of paper.

"What are you up to?" asked Jake.

"Oh, I hope you don't mind, but I was moving some of your books and I realized I was holding your math assignment in my hand. So I thought I might as well get started on it."

Jake looked at the paper. "It looks like you finished."

"I'm pretty good at math," said Nathan. "Do you have any other homework to do?"

"No," said Jake, "but I'd better copy over what you did so it at least looks like I did it."

"Oh, sure," said Nathan. "Here, I'll get out of your way."

Jake sat down at the desk. The paper looked like his handwriting, exactly. Jake said, "This looks like I did it."

Nathan said, "But correctly. Now what do we do?"

"Watch TV?"

Nathan said, "No, you don't want to do that. How about we go play some basketball."

"Sure," said Jake, "anything you say."

Chapter 14

When Margery hung up the phone she blurted out, "Jake's created his double." Just then a shadow came in through the window, went into one of Margery's ears, and came out the other. "That's funny," Margery said. "I could have sworn that I just said Jake created his bubble. What does that mean? I'm flipping out." The shadow left the room.

Margery met Nathan the next day at school. Margery was waiting on the front steps at the main entrance.

Margery said, "Hi, Jake," to Nathan and then she said to Jake, "You must be Jake's cousin, Nathan. Nice to meet you. I'm one of Jake's friends. My name is Margery. I go to this school, too. I'm a year older than Jake. We're kind of good friends. Has he told you? Do you know his brother Sam? That's stupid, of course you know his brother." She laughed. "You're all staying at the same house."

"Nice to meet you," said Jake, "but I already know you. I'm Jake."

Margery said, "Incredible, you look so much alike. It makes me sort of dizzy to look at you."

"Everyone says that," said Nathan. "I'm looking forward to getting to know you. A friend of Jake's is a friend of mine. We'll have to all three get together sometime. Maybe we could do something fun after school."

"Sounds good to me," said Margery. She then asked Jake, "Did you tell him about the book?"

Jake tried to kill her with a look.

"What book is that?" asked Nathan.

"Yes, what book?" said Jake with his teeth clenched.

Margery stuttered for a minute and then said, "Oh, we were thinking about writing a book together, and we were kind of writing it after school and stuff. You know it isn't that big a deal so just forget I even mentioned it."

Nathan said, "Jake, you are full of surprises. I hate to drop the subject but I'm supposed to check in at the office. Jake's dad has arranged everything for me to visit but I'm still supposed to check in. So if you'll excuse us, Margery, we will see you this afternoon."

"Oh, right," said Margery. "I'm sorry. I'll see you later. I mean if I see one of you I guess I'll see the other." She sat down. "I'm dizzy again."

She sat and watched them going through the doors. She thought that Jake looked blurry. It was the only way she could describe it. It was like bad TV reception. "Maybe it is because I'm so dizzy," thought Margery. Margery didn't know.

Her palms were sweaty and her face felt hot.

"His eyes," she thought. "He did something with his eyes. I couldn't think when he was looking at me."

Just then a girl from Jake's class came up and said, "Margery have you seen Jake's cousin? He looks just like Jake except he's cute."

Margery said, "He's not that cute."

The girl said, "Maybe it will rub off on Jake, at least a little. He could use some of it. You have to admit."

Margery didn't answer; she started walking to class. "I'm still dizzy," she said.

She stopped walking and three people behind her crashed directly into her. "Sorry," Margery said.

"I'm flipping out," said Margery to herself while picking up her books and papers. "Maybe I should go see the school nurse. Maybe I'm the one getting blurry. I've got to relax. I'm under too much pressure."

Just then the bell rang and Margery

headed for her geography class. In their first class of the day, Spanish, Nathan and Jake had just finished talking to the teacher, Mrs. Lamper. "Sit where you like," she said to Nathan. "We don't assign seats."

Nathan took a seat in front of Jake. "This way I can let you hide and take a nap."

"Perfect," said Jake.

"Did I tell you I'm a ventriloquist?" said Nathan. "I could even answer for you."

"Even more perfect," said Jake.

Nathan did. Jake would raise his hand and Nathan would answer the question. Jake could hardly sit in his seat he was laughing so hard. The teacher couldn't get over the change in Jake, that is, until she started getting dizzy.

Mrs. Lamper said, "Excuse me class, I seem to be dizzy. Study your dialogues for this week while I get a hold of myself."

Mrs. Lamper couldn't stand being dizzy. In exactly three minutes she blew chips into her wastebasket in front of the whole class. Three other kids blew chips right after her because they had to watch her.

Mrs. Lamper said, "I don't know what came over me."

The principal came into their room and sent them all outside while the janitors cleaned up and sprayed some stuff in the air.

On the way out of class someone asked the principal what the Spanish word for *barf* was and got an hour and a half of detention.

The day continued. Everywhere Jake and Nathan went, someone got dizzy and everyone got confused. Whenever Jake got called on in class Nathan answered and answered correctly.

The teachers all said, "Jake, that can't be you. Can it?"

"Yes, of course," Nathan would say.

Jake had the giggles most of the day. "This is so great," he thought. "Who needs a double when they have Nathan?"

Jake didn't go to PE. Nathan told him to hide out in the boiler room and he'd go for him. Jake hated PE since he'd been called the mop. That day they were playing basketball and Nathan calling himself Jake made twenty-eight points. The PE instructor kept saying, "Hey, Stone, what'd you have for breakfast?"

Nathan got up in English and gave an oral book report on a book he'd never read. Jake hadn't read it either so he had nothing to lose by letting Nathan give it. Nathan got an A.

"Nathan, you're terrific," said Jake. "I hope you never leave."

"You need me, don't you, Jake?" said Nathan. "I'm everything you're not. You hate yourself, don't you, Jake?"

"Yes," said Jake, "but I like you."

Jake had stopped trying to create his double. Instead, he was now trying to walk like Nathan, talk like Nathan, be Nathan.

Chapter 15

Margery could only see it from a distance, but she was close enough to know what was going on. She had just come out of the school. Across the parking lot and the street she could see a bunch of kids forming a circle.

She knew it was a fight. If you had a fight you always went across the street. Everyone said that teachers couldn't do anything to you if you were off the school grounds. It wasn't true, but they said it anyway. Anytime there was a fight, across the street or not, a teacher always stopped it or at least found out about it and punished the kids involved.

"I wonder who is so stupid to start a fight?" Margery said.

The circle across the street opened for a second and then she saw. It looked like Nathan and he was punching the stuffing out out of someone. By the time she ran across the street, it was over. She heard the other

guy say, "I'm sorry. I'll never say it again."
She noticed Jake or Nathan and went over
and stood by him. He was standing there
totally embarrassed, not knowing what to do.

It was Nathan who had been fighting and
who was now shaking hands with the other
guy and saying, "Friends?"

Jake sort of slithered away from the group.
He hadn't seen Margery standing next to him.
Margery followed him and as he left the
circle of kids she grabbed him by the shirt.
He jumped a foot and without looking at who
it was yelled, "What do you want?"

"I want to know what went on."

"Nathan got in a fight."

"No kidding," said Margery. "Over what?"
Jake didn't answer.

"Over what?" repeated Margery.

"Well, I guess you could say it was over
me."

"What?" said Margery raising her eyebrows
above the top rim of her glasses.

Jake started mumbling. "Dick was just saying some things to me that I usually ignore,
but then Nathan — "

Just then Nathan came up behind them. "I
hope that wasn't uncomfortable," he said to
Jake. "I can be quite good at fighting, and that
guy deserved to be knocked down a couple of
notches."

"Oh, no," said Jake. "It was fine. Thanks."

Nathan patted him on the shoulder.

Jake started to say, "It's just that I could have done it myself," but Nathan was also saying, "I just figure that if someone says something about you they say it about me, and I won't stand for it." He had a big grin on his face. He looked at Margery. "Well, what do we do now?"

Jake said, "I think I'd better go home."

"You're kidding!" said Nathan.

"No, I don't feel good. I must have had something bad at lunch. You two go ahead. I'll just go home and lie down for a while."

Margery said, "You're not dizzy are you? There's a lot of it going around."

"No," said Jake to Margery. Then to Nathan he said, "Thanks, Nathan. I wish I'd been able to do it. I'm such a jerk and you're everything I'm not."

"You don't look good," said Margery, "you look sort of weak."

"Thanks, that makes me feel great," said Jake.

"Ah c'mon, Jake," said Nathan, "it'll be all right. You'll see. Just let me take over for you. I mean take care of you."

"I wish I was you," said Jake, "or you were me."

"Really?" said Nathan.

"Really?" said Margery.

"Ya," said Jake. "I'd be smart and tough and look even more like you."

"You're sort of smart and sort of tough

and you definitely look like him," said Margery.

Nathan looked in Jake's eyes and smiled.

"I guess I'll go home. You guys have fun," said Jake. He walked away from the school.

Margery felt something. She wasn't just dizzy. She felt something tugging on her. It wanted her to follow Jake. Then just as suddenly as it started it stopped.

Nathan turned to Margery. "What do you think? You want to go bowling?"

"Gee, I don't know," said Margery. She was a little worried about doing things with Nathan. Partially for reasons she didn't understand and partially because doing things with Jake was okay because they practically grew up together, but doing something with Nathan was more like going out, or even a date.

She thought for a minute. "Oh, why not," she said. "I'm a horrible bowler but what the heck."

"Oh great, so am I," said Nathan.

"Somehow I don't believe it," said Margery.

Chapter 16

That night when Nathan got home, Jake was in bed.

Jake's mom said, "I think he'll be all right, Nathan, but I have been worried about him. He's been so tired lately. I guess growing up takes it out of you. Where do you get your energy?"

Without thinking Nathan answered, "Jake."

"Oh?" said Jake's mother. "I don't understand."

"I mean," said Nathan, "I mean . . . well, I guess it doesn't really matter."

"Oh," repeated Jake's mother, feeling another dizzy spell coming on.

"I guess I'll go up and see how he is," said Nathan.

"You're so considerate, Nathan."

"I'm trying to be," said Nathan.

"We're enjoying your being here. It's nice for Jake to have someone close to his age to live with. To watch you two together, you'd think you were identical twins. I always thought having a twin would be fun."

"Me, too," said Nathan.

"I just wish we all felt better," said Jake's mother.

Nathan said, "I have a feeling you'll be better soon." He went upstairs, and Jake's mother lay down on the floor.

"It's the only thing that helps," she said.

"How you doing, Jake?" asked Nathan.

"I'm okay," answered Jake. "I just felt weak."

"You should stay in bed. It will make you go faster . . . I mean get well faster."

"Nathan, I know this may sound dumb, but I was thinking about today and all the stuff you did for me and nobody has really ever done things like that for me before and I just don't understand. Do you like me? I mean if I wasn't family would you like me?"

"It all depends," laughed Nathan. "Let us say I am very grateful for the opportunity you have offered me."

"But do you like me?" asked Jake.

"It's my theory that all this like and love stuff is just a lie. People need each other to accomplish certain things. That is all. They make up this affection stuff to make them feel more important than they are. Do you understand what I'm saying?"

"No," said Jake.

"But it will make you like me more if I say I like you?" asked Nathan.

"Ya," said Jake, "I guess so."

"Then fine Jake. I like you."

Jake shivered. Suddenly the room was very cold.

"Your mom even says we look and act like twins. We've sure got 'em fooled," said Nathan.

"Ya," agreed Jake.

"We'll have to think of even more fun ways to confuse everyone. You'll have to let me pretend to be you more. Think of the laughs," said Nathan.

"If I get any weaker you'll have to be me completely," said Jake.

Nathan laughed. "Seems you get weaker and I just feel stronger. Watch this." Nathan stood on his hands and did ten push-ups.

"Awesome," said Jake. "You are so great."

Nathan laughed some more.

Jake said, "Nathan, can I tell you a secret?"

"Me?" said Nathan. "Of course. You shouldn't hold anything back from your twin."

"Before you arrived I was trying to create my double using this book. Does that sound stupid?"

"Very," said Nathan. "How were you supposed to do it?"

"With my mind," said Jake, laughing. "Isn't that funny?"

"Your mind?" said Nathan, "Your mind is nothing. That is funny. Remember that what you have is all there is. That's my motto."

"Right," said Jake.

"Besides," said Nathan, "you don't need a double. You've got your cousin Nathan."

"Right again," said Jake.

"You need me, don't you, Jake?"

"I sure do," said Jake.

Chapter 17

The next day Jake thought he felt a little better.

"Take care of him, Nathan," Jake's mom said, sending them out the door.

"You can count on me," said Nathan.

"Improve his grades," said Jake's dad.

"Yes, sir," laughed Nathan.

On the way to school Jake said, "I guess my dad cares about me, but he sure shows it in funny ways."

Nathan said, "Forget it, Jake. I learned long, long ago that nobody cares about you except yourself . . . parents especially."

"Oh, ya," said Jake, wanting Nathan to approve of him. "I agree."

"You don't need anybody, Jake. I mean if you let them, everyone just uses you and treats you like dirt. I mean that's how I feel. Don't you?"

"Exactly," said Jake. "You're better off not even talking to people."

"Except me," said Nathan.

"Of course," said Jake, "and probably Margery."

"Can't trust girls, Jake."

"But she's my friend."

"Lies, Jake. Grow up. This is the real world," said Nathan.

"Can we rest a minute?" asked Jake. "I'm feeling weak again."

"No problem," said Nathan. "On second thought, rest as long as you want. I'll go to school as you and when you come in, you be me. Visitors don't get into trouble for being late."

"Okay, I suppose it would work," said Jake.

Nathan did it. He was Jake and Jake was Nathan. They continued switching all day long until Jake didn't know who he was.

Nathan was Jake for his class picture. "I look better than you today," said Nathan.

In science he was Jake to take a test Jake hadn't studied for. In PE they were doing ballroom dancing, and Nathan pretended he was Jake and even danced with the teacher. He bowed to her at the end of the dance.

Ms. Jensen said, "Jake, you've turned into a regular Prince Charming."

"Would you like another dance?" asked Nathan.

"I'd love to," she said, "but I'm kind of dizzy."

Jake was behind a post howling.

All the girls were saying, "Jake, oh, Jake, can you be my partner next?"

"Look at that," thought Jake. "Even that dumb Jennifer wants to dance with me."

Chapter 18

The next weeks marked major changes for Jake and his family. First Jake's dad put railings up everywhere in the house.

"The place looks like a huge ballet studio," said Jake.

Jake's dad did it because everyone was so dang dizzy all the time. The doctor had checked them all out but found nothing wrong. "It must be some side effect of the flu that is going around," he said. "Call me if it doesn't get better."

Jake kept getting weaker. He started missing school. At first he thought it would be fun to skip but then it seemed like he had to stay home. He didn't have the energy to go. "Don't worry," said Nathan. "You don't need yourself. You've got me. I keep telling you I'll take care of you."

"It's true," thought Jake. "Who needs Jake Stone when they could have Nathan?"

Nathan told some people he was Nathan and other people he was Jake. He told the school people that he was Jake and that Nathan had left. That way Jake didn't get into trouble for being at home.

One day Jake's mother said, "I'm so confused. I can't seem to remember who is Jake and who is Nathan. Oh, well," she continued, "I'm so dizzy I don't know what time it is either."

One night, Jake's dad came into Jake's room and said, "For some reason I've missed you all day Jake. I kept thinking you'd left and it made me sad. Must be because I'm so dizzy."

Jake's sister seemed to be the only one not affected by Nathan. She said, "Nathan, why don't you get rid of Jake and just move in permanently?"

"Would you like that?" said Nathan.

"Give me a break, Nathan."

She was thoroughly embarrassed because of the bars going all through the house. The only way she could invite people over was to tell them that her dad did it so she could practice her ballet wherever she was. When people came over she did at least fifty pliés while talking to them. "If this keeps up," she thought, "I'm going to have the biggest thighs in the world. My family is so embarrassing."

Sam said he was only dizzy at home so he spent more time at Joanie's and the pool.

"That's fine, dear," said Sam's mother when Sam said he wouldn't be home for dinner, "I'm too dizzy to cook anyway."

The month continued and Nathan kept taking Jake's place until Jake stopped coming out of his room. "I hate myself for being so tired," said Jake. "Nathan, I can't seem to get up anymore. Can you be me until I'm better?"

"I'll try," said Nathan.

People would call to ask for Jake and Nathan would answer the phone.

Suddenly Jake had a terrifying thought: "It's like I don't live here anymore." He looked at his hand and it totally disappeared for a second. "I'm fading," he told Nathan.

"Getting fainter every day, Jake old boy. Now wasn't it easier than you thought it would be?"

"What?" said Jake, taking a deep breath.

"Hey," said Nathan, "don't breathe so deep, it'll just get in the way."

"What was easier?" asked Jake.

"Aw c'mon," said Nathan. "You remember . . . me!"

"I don't get it," said Jake.

"And that is why you deserve me, Jake. You had the power to create your double and you did it. Now you don't even realize it."

"I did? Really?" said Jake.

"Jake, you are even stupider than *you* think. Now relax. It's almost over. You're getting what you wanted. It was simple, easy.

I'm sort of enjoying being you. Sort of. Don't let the wind blow you away," said Nathan.

"It can't be true," thought Jake. "It just can't."

Then he got real scared. He started thinking about the things Nathan had said. He got to thinking about all the times Nathan was being Jake. "Oh, no," Jake said. "What do I do now? I'm such a jerk. I need help. Nathan, you can't do this to me. You are my friend."

"It is either me or you, Jake, and it's going to be me," said Nathan, leaving the room and slamming the door behind him.

Chapter 19

Margery had just finished washing her hair in the shower, the real way with shampoo and lots and lots of water. She had done just what the book said to do.

> *When there is a task that worries you or makes you feel frightened, stop pushing yourself. You will only increase your fear. Stop looking at the entire problem. Stop trying to solve everything at once. Do only what you can. Do only what you can and then do a little bit more. Then do a little bit more until you have built little success upon little success and you find you have reached your goal. Remember, you will succeed because you always get what you want.*

What Margery had done first was pour a

glass of water on her head. Then the next day she had poured a pitcher of water over her head. Both days she survived it by breathing deeply while doing it. She had found that part of her panic was that she had stopped breathing whenever she was near water. It is smart to hold your breath when you are fully underwater, but to hold your breath when you look at water is crazy.

The book had said:

> *It is very common for people to stop breathing when they are doing something they are afraid of. Do not let yourself do this. Holding your breath is the last thing you should do. What you need to do is breathe more. Breathe deep and full. If you can do nothing else while you are feeling fear, breathe. Remember, fear is a thought in your mind and breathing has the power to keep it from taking over your body.*

Margery had done it and it worked. She was still afraid, but it felt different. It felt different enough that she wanted to go on. She did go on. Next she actually washed her hair in the sink and then she washed it in the shower. She even caught herself singing in the shower.

"It helps me breathe," she told herself.

Her mother was so happy. "I just can't believe what nice care you are giving your
hair. You are such a beautiful girl when you
let yourself be that way."

Margery had said, "Right, Mom," like she
didn't care but it had gotten right to her. She
even looked in the mirror once and said to
herself that she thought her mother was right.
She was beautiful.

Margery was feeling a new sense of con-
fidence. She felt like she could do anything.
She said, "It was so easy. Why didn't I do it
ages ago?" She now even felt like taking
swimming lessons. "I feel like it but not yet,"
she wrote in her diary. "Besides there is no
use in taking them while I am so busy with
Nathan."

She had a lot about Nathan in her diary.
Flipping through the pages she saw the entry
where she went bowling the first time with
Nathan. She read it over.

Dear Diary,
I went bowling with Nathan today
after school. He even paid for me so
it was kind of like a date, but I
would just die if anyone said any-
thing to me about it or called it that.
Anyway, he is so good at everything
and so funny. I just can't believe it.
It was too bad that Jake couldn't go

with us. Writing this now I feel bad he didn't go with us, but when I was with Nathan I never even gave it a thought. I feel a little guilty about that. Oh, well, the next time I see Jake I'll tell him he should take some vitamins. Nathan is so cute! You just wouldn't believe he would want to be my friend.

Margery couldn't believe it when she read the date. It had almost been a month ago when she wrote that entry. From that date she noticed that almost every entry said something about Nathan. Something about where they had been together and what they had done. None of them said anything about Jake. It was like he had disappeared out of her life for a month. She looked back through past months and there he was, but when Nathan appeared he just stopped.

Nathan always said Jake didn't feel good. It wasn't like Margery hadn't tried to include him. It was just that he was always so tired.

Inside Margery's mind something was pushing her. Actually it was pushing and pulling her. "Call Jake," it would say. Then another voice would say, "Forget about Jake."

She wrote down in her diary, "Talk to Jake or call him tomorrow. Act like a friend."

With that she went to sleep for the night.

She had a dream. It was probably more like a nightmare. Jake was in a bird cage. He was small. He was the size of a parakeet.

"What are you doing in the cage?" Margery said.

Jake said nothing.

Just then Nathan came into the room, picked up a pair of tweezers, and plucked a feather from Jake's body. He then left the room laughing.

Margery woke up sweating. "What does that mean?" she wondered.

The dream stuck with her all through breakfast. "Something is wrong with Jake," she told herself. Her mother even noticed her concern.

"Anything wrong, Margery?" her mother asked.

"I don't think so. It's just that I haven't seen much of Jake lately."

"I thought you were spending lots of time with him."

"That's his mother's cousin," said Margery. "His name is Nathan."

"Could have fooled me."

Chapter 20

Margery found Nathan in between classes. "Where's Jake?" she said, almost attacking him.

"Who?" said Nathan. "I'm Jake."

"Forget it, Nathan. I know Jake. I may be the only one that really knows Jake."

"Well, I haven't locked him up, if that's what you think," answered Nathan. He looked into her eyes.

"Oh, sorry, Nathan," she said looking back into Nathan's eyes. They're such a nice color, she told herself. She paused and then asked Nathan, "What was I talking about?"

"Something about us going to the mall tonight to just hang out."

"I was? Oh, ya, now I remember."

Just then a guy named Max came by and said, "Hi Margery, hi Jake, here's the money you lent me yesterday."

Margery shook her head. It was like there

was a big fluffy marshmallow stuck between her ears.

After Max had left she repeated to Nathan, "Where is Jake?" This time she was digging through her book bag and not looking in Nathan's eyes.

"Still sick or sick again," said Nathan. "Anyway, he stayed at home. It's actually just as well. I pick up his schoolwork, help him with it, and then return it for him. The more he's missed of school the better his grades have gotten."

"What's wrong with him?" asked Margery, now digging through some papers.

"I don't know. He'll probably be back tomorrow. Now about tonight."

"Listen, we'd better skip tonight. My folks don't like me to go to the mall and besides I think I should go see Jake."

Nathan moved, pulling Margery to the side of the hall. "Look at me," said Nathan. "He's just fine. He'd like us to have a good time. When he feels better he'll join us. It's okay. I'll pick you up at seven. I'll make, I mean, I'll get Sam to drive us. It'll be great."

"Oh, ya," said Margery, looking straight at Nathan, "sounds good."

"Well, I have to go to class. See you tonight."

"Sure," said Margery.

Margery stood there trying to remember something important. It had to do with something she wanted to say to somebody or something she had to go do or somebody who was in trouble. She couldn't remember. "Whatever it was," she said to herself, "it couldn't have been too important, or I would have remembered it."

Then, like a match being lit in a dark gymnasium, a small voice inside her brain said, "Jake." "Jake," she said out loud but right then it meant nothing to her.

Chapter 21

Margery had the same parakeet dream. "I've got to see Jake." She woke up screaming.

Jake was sick again. He wasn't at school. She didn't talk to Nathan except to say hi at lunch. "You don't have to be unfriendly," she said to herself, but she still didn't want to be around him. She felt she was being silly. She told herself it was just the dream. She'd done it before. She'd dreamt about someone and then when she saw him she couldn't forget what he had done in her dream. Inside her she did not want to be around Nathan. The feeling was strong.

As soon as she got home she tried to call Jake.

"Hi, Margery," Sam said as he answered the phone. "Sure you can talk to Jake. Just a second."

"This is Jake," said the voice on the other end of the line.

"Very funny, Nathan," said Margery, "I need to talk to Jake."

"Oh," said Nathan, "Sam said it was for me."

Margery tried to laugh.

"How are you doing?" said Nathan.

"Great. We had fun last night."

"I didn't think you did, the way you were avoiding me today."

"Oh, that," said Margery. "I just had this dream."

"You did?" said Nathan. "About me?"

"Ya, sort of."

"Tell me about it," demanded Nathan.

The feeling was back. Something or someone in her said, "Don't say anything. Something is wrong."

"Oh, it was no big deal."

"Really?" asked Nathan.

"Actually it wasn't even about you. Really it wasn't about anything. I've just been trying to concentrate, and I find you so distracting." Margery almost laughed, listening to herself. "How's school? You have any homework?"

"Hardly any," said Nathan.

There was a long pause. Margery was waiting for him to say, "I'll go get Jake," but he didn't.

"Well, can I talk to Jake?" she finally said.

"Who?" said Nathan.

"You know, the guy you live with."

Nathan just laughed.

"Hello?" said Margery.

"Want to go swimming after dinner? Or

maybe wash your hair?" asked Nathan.

"What?" said Margery.

"Oh, nothing," said Nathan.

"That creep Jake," Margery thought, "he's told him everything." "I'm busy tonight," said Margery.

"Up to you," said Nathan. Then he laughed again. Margery had never noticed his laugh before. It sounded mean, almost sinister.

Margery got off the phone. Her dad was standing there. "You look like you just saw a ghost," he said.

"He sure acted weird," said Margery.

"Who is that?"

"Jake, I mean Nathan," said Margery, shaking her head.

"It's easy to get those two confused," said her dad. "I saw Jake and Nathan with Jake's mother at the grocery store, and I couldn't tell them apart. I told them the resemblance was remarkable. Jake's mother said she was just thrilled having Nathan around the house. It had just changed everything for her. Isn't it nice he's fitted in so well?"

"When was that Dad? When you saw them together?" asked Margery.

"Gosh, must have been a month ago."

"Wonderful," said Margery. The voice in her kept saying, "See Jake." She knew something was seriously wrong and she had to get to him.

At Jake's house, Nathan had just announced that he thought he had just about worn out his welcome and that he should return home.

"That's silly," said Jake's mother. "This is your home."

Nathan said, "Aren't you a little tired of having an extra mouth to feed and someone else to look after?"

"I don't know what you're talking about," said Jake's mother.

Upstairs, Jake was in bed. He was still feeling very, very weak and he thought something was wrong with his eyesight. The doctor had seen him that day but he couldn't find anything organic. "Probably still some kind of flu bug," the doctor had said. "He'll get over it in a couple of weeks. Just keep him in bed."

Nathan came into the room and looked at Jake in bed. "We'll be leaving soon. I mean you'll be leaving soon."

Jake could only nod. Whenever Nathan was in the same room with him now he couldn't even talk.

"Not room for two marshals in this town, pardner," Nathan said in a cowboy drawl. "Meet you at high noon, or I think I prefer high midnight." Nathan threw his head back and howled like a wolf. Then he laughed and laughed and laughed.

Chapter 22

Margery called the school. "This is Mrs. Stone," she said, holding her nose to sound older, "Jake Stone's mother."

"Yes, Mrs. Stone," the receptionist said, "I was about to leave, but what can I do for you?"

"Sorry for calling so late, but I wanted to know how many days of school Jake has missed in the last month. It's been a few, and I've lost count. You know, the doctor was asking me and — "

The receptionist laughed. Margery thought that the receptionist knew who she was. However, Margery didn't know that this receptionist always laughed out of relief when parents called, and she found out they didn't want to complain about something.

Margery was ready to hang up when the receptionist said, "It'll just take me a second. Let me take a look." There was a pause as she found the record. "Yes," she said, "here he is. Oh, my goodness, he hasn't missed a day this month. There must be a mistake. He's listed here as having perfect attendance."

"Sorry, my mistake," said Margery, "wrong school." She slammed down the receiver.

Margery didn't know what to do. She knew Jake had missed a lot of school. Then she felt super guilty because she hadn't thought about it, hadn't even cared. "Where have I been?" she said. "It's like I've been under a spell or something."

She was standing there feeling guilty and wondering what to do next when the phone rang. She picked up the receiver and said hello at least eight times. All she could hear was someone breathing. "Is this an obscene phone call?" she asked.

Then if she hadn't been listening extra careful she would have missed it. Ever so faintly she heard, "I created my double." It was Jake.

"What? Jake, is that you?" said Margery, but the phone was dead.

She flew out of her house and ran down to Jake's. She knocked on the door and Mrs. Stone opened it.

"Could I see Jake?" she asked. "It's important."

"Jake isn't home right now," said Mrs. Stone.

Margery looked at Mrs. Stone's eyes. The

pupils were large and she looked as if she were watching something very far away.

"Mrs. Stone I really need to see Jake, you know, your son!"

"I know," said Mrs. Stone, "but Jake isn't home right now."

Margery just stood there. Finally she said, "Okay, I'll come back. Fine."

"How nice, Margery. I'll tell Nathan you stopped by."

"Nathan?" Margery asked.

"I mean Jake," said Jake's mother.

"Don't bother telling him," said Margery.

Margery went around the house and looked up at Jake's window. "I know you're in there," she whispered.

The only thing she could do was sneak into the house or climb up and go through the window. She tried the back door and it was locked. The only way to get to the window was to climb a tree. That involved heights.

Margery told herself, "I can do anything! I'll just keep breathing and I'll make it."

She put one foot in front of the other and started climbing.

"This isn't so bad," she said to herself, and then she looked down.

She almost passed out from fright. "Stop it!" she said. She slipped twice, but each time she kept telling herself she could succeed and even if she fell she would get right back up and climb till she reached the window.

Breathing heavily she moved right up and into Jake's window.

"Ta Da!" she practically screamed as she came in. She felt great. She was Wonder Woman, Supergirl, able to do anything she set her mind to.

"Shhh," she said to herself. Then she looked over at Jake's bed. There he was, or at least she thought he was. Jake looked almost transparent. He was fading away.

"You're not yourself lately are you, Jake?" she said, not even thinking that it wasn't the time to make jokes. It didn't matter however, because she couldn't tell whether he could hear her or not. She couldn't even tell if he could see her or not. She went over to his bed.

"Margery, you came," he said, sounding very hollow and almost ready to cry.

"Of course," she said. "How are you feeling? If you don't mind my saying so, you look worse. I mean like totally awful."

"I'm fading," said Jake, now almost sobbing.

"I noticed," said Margery. "This is crazy. People don't fade. Do your parents know?"

"He's got them under some kind of spell. He's taking over. He's replacing me. I did create my double and now he is destroying me."

"Who?" asked Margery. "Nathan?"

"Yes," he said.

Margery said, "It really works, doesn't it?"

Jake said, "It works."

"It works good, it works bad. You have to pick good things to want."

"I know," said Jake. "I didn't."

"What do we do?" asked Margery. "What do we do?"

"Help me!" said Jake. He started fading a little more.

"Hang on!" said Margery. "I'll do something. We have to be brave."

She stood and thought. She bit her fingernails. She twirled her clean hair around her finger.

Finally she said, "I need the book. I need that dang book. Oh, no! I took the book back to the library. It was overdue. I solved my hair problem and I didn't need it anymore. I have to go to the library and get it. What day is it? Let me see, Wednesday. Oh, no! What time is it? The library closes at five on Wednesdays. What'll we do?"

She looked at Jake. "Breathe, Jake," she said. "You have to breathe. Breathe deeply while I get help."

Jake started breathing deeply into his chest. Margery was sure every time he inhaled he seemed clearer.

"Keep breathing!" she said and she headed out the window.

Chapter 23

Margery went down the tree easily. She didn't think about it. Her mind was busy. She just couldn't believe what she had seen.

"Maybe I need my glasses changed," she thought. Then the thought came to her that maybe she could get herself to not need glasses by just thinking about it. "Later, Margery," she told herself.

She ran home. Now, it was after five. She thought about calling the librarian at home, but she was such a crab. Margery didn't want to bother her, but she also didn't know what else to do. She needed the book.

"Mrs. Smith?" Margery said.

"Yes, what is it?"

"This is Margery."

"Margery?"

"Yes, Margery Wake."

"Oh, hello, Margery."

"Mrs. Smith I have a favor to ask of you."

"What do you have in mind, Margery? Do you have some raffle tickets to sell? I usually don't buy them and I was trying to get dinner started — or rather I was helping my husband, you know, he's such a marvelous cook."

"It's about the book *Change Your Mind and You Can Change Your World.*"

"Yes, I'm so glad you brought it back in."

"Well, I need it back again right now."

"Whatever for? Didn't you finish it? You've renewed it at least four times."

"Well, well, I need it to write a book report, and I forgot to get some stuff out of it."

"I see," said Mrs. Smith.

"Could I possibly meet you there and pick it up?"

"I'm sorry, Margery, but you would have to place a reserve on the title. I remember checking it out. It happened to be the last book I checked out today. I'm really not supposed to disclose who checked out the book, but it was one of your friends and perhaps you could call him up and ask him for the information."

"Who was it?" asked Margery.

"Your friend Nathan. You know he looks so much like Jake Stone. In fact I thought it was Jake until Nathan signed his name."

"Thanks, Mrs. Smith," said Margery.

Margery hung up and staring at the phone said, "Now what?" There was nothing she could do except get back to Jake.

She ran out the door. "Time for dinner," her mother called behind her.

"I'll be right back," answered Margery.

Nathan was standing over Jake's bed. "Looks to me like you only have about an hour left. I'll tell them you left. You caught a cab. You couldn't stand to say good-bye. No more Jake. You're now Nathan. I'm Jake now, and I'll do a lot better job at it than you did. Don't worry. They'll forget Nathan even existed in a very short time. It will all be very natural."

Jake could only stare up at him.

Nathan left the room. "It's dinnertime," he said. "I have to make sure I keep them all confused as to what is going on here."

Jake could barely see the clock. Where was Margery? How long had she been gone? He couldn't speak the words. He could only think them. "Someone help me, please!"

Margery was running back to Jake's. "I'll convince his parents. I'll make them understand. I'll stop him that way." Then she remembered Mrs. Stone's eyes and what she had said. She knew she would never convince her in time. She had to assume that Sam and Jake's dad were in the same position. She thought maybe Jake's sister could help, but then she realized she didn't seem to care about either Jake or Nathan.

She panicked. "Nathan had me in the same way. He made me forget about Jake."

She had been under the spell, too. When she was with Nathan, Jake never even entered her mind.

"I've got to stay away from him."

Margery then started to climb the tree in front of Jake's bedroom window. It didn't even cross her mind that she was afraid of heights.

Chapter 24

Margery reached Jake's window, but this time it was closed. Looking at it she realized it was not only shut but also locked. "Oh, no," was all she could say.

Beneath her she heard an odd sound. It sounded like a huge lawn mower or maybe a chain saw. She looked down.

"Oh, my goodness!" she tried to say but nothing came out.

Nathan looked up at her with a chain saw in his hand. "Thought I'd do a little bit of pruning," he yelled.

Before she could even think or scream for help, Margery used her foot to kick in Jake's window. She then reached in and unlocked it. Quickly she scrambled into the room, trying to avoid any major lacerations.

She ran and locked Jake's door and pushed his desk and the dresser in front of it. She then threw herself toward Jake's bed. He was barely a ghost now.

First she took a couple of deep breaths to calm herself down as much as possible, and then she spoke to what was left of Jake. "You created this and you can uncreate it. All you have to do is face it. All you have to do is create your own self back. Muster up everything you have. Take hold of yourself. You can do it. You can be yourself again. Love yourself."

Just then Nathan started banging on the door. "Don't you think I can destroy this house if I want to?" he screamed from out in the hall. "Stop, Jake. Remember you hate yourself."

"That's it, Jake. That's it," said Margery. "You have to love yourself."

"You're an idiot, Jake," said Nathan. "You're stupid. You were nothing without me. You don't deserve to be anything."

"Jake," said Margery. "You can't listen to him. It's not true."

"Yes, it is," said Jake. "I'm a worm."

"Jake," started Margery, "you're being stupid as usual! Oh, no, what am I doing? Jake, you're not being stupid. You just have to stop."

"Jake," boomed Nathan, "you know you hate yourself. You've got every reason in the world. You're a nerd, Jake, a nerd. You're stupid. You're clumsy. You're dirt, Jake. You're nothing. Everyone hates you. You're family doesn't care about you."

"Shut up!" yelled Margery. "You're lying. Stop it."

Nathan said through the door, "Margery, don't think I won't get you, too. I already have. Admit it. You liked me a whole lot more than Jake. A whole lot more. You wanted me to be your boyfriend, didn't you Margery?"

Margery was feeling dizzy. "Well," she said.

"We can, Margery. I'll be your boyfriend. I'll do anything you ask. Just let me in. You'll forget about Jake. He'll be all right. You'll see. It won't hurt him."

"Please — please stop," said Margery.

"Let me in, Margery," said Nathan.

"No, no, no," said Margery.

"I suppose not by the clean hair of your chinny chin chin?" said Nathan.

"Get away," said Margery.

"Fun and games are over," yelled Nathan.

The room started shaking. Margery looked toward the door. The dresser was vibrating and both it and the desk were quickly moving away from the door. The door flew open and in walked Nathan. He stood there and laughed. "You're too late. Look at him. He's not there anymore. He hates himself too much."

Margery turned to Jake. "I can't do it for you. You created this. You have to uncreate it."

Jake thought as hard as he could. The only

thing that came to mind was what a jerk he was to have done this to himself.

Margery knew what he was thinking and yelled at him. "You made a mistake. Admit it and forgive yourself. Forgive yourself, stupid. I mean you aren't stupid, but forgive yourself! It's okay. What is done in the past is done. Love yourself right now. It was just a mistake. It's okay to make mistakes."

Jake started in. He tried to "unthink" Nathan.

"That's it," said Nathan, "think about me. Think about how you wanted me."

"This was all a mistake," thought Jake. "I didn't mean it."

"You're calling me a mistake, Jake? You are the mistake!" said Nathan.

Jake looked at Nathan, but Nathan wasn't moving his lips. He was talking inside Jake's head.

"I'm part of you now, Jake. You can't get rid of me."

"Don't think about him, Jake!" yelled Margery. "Think about the good parts of yourself!"

Jake mustered all his courage. "Nathan," he thought, "you were a mistake."

Nathan just laughed.

Jake continued, "I thought I wanted you, but I don't."

"That's what you think!" said Nathan.

"I don't need you Nathan because I can do

things myself. I can talk for myself. I can take my own tests. I can make my own friends."

"Not without me you can't," said Nathan. "You'll flunk. Everyone will make fun of you."

"I don't care," said Jake. "Sure I may be funny and do some things wrong . . . but it's okay because I'm trying, and I'll get better and stronger. I've got good points. I care about things. I'm nice to people."

"Keep it up," said Margery, "that's it."

"You shut up," said Nathan, throwing Margery into the closet just by thinking about it. Just before the door slammed shut and locked he said to Margery, "See what you can do if you just think about it?"

Jake tried to continue. Nathan was humming in his brain.

"I can't do it," said Jake. "It's too noisy inside me."

"You don't like my funeral music?" said Nathan.

Jake forced himself. "I'm thinking good things about myself. I'm nice to animals, and I love sunsets and" —

Nathan started to sing both inside and outside his head.

— "I love to sing in the church choir, and I love my mom and dad and my brother and my sister. I don't want to be Nathan or anyone else. I want to be myself. My nerdy, ugly self who does things wrong but keeps on going . . . who has fun no matter what and likes trees to climb and how the world looks from twenty feet up."

"It won't work," yelled Nathan.

"No matter what happens," yelled Margery, "I love you, Jake. I'll always be your friend."

With all his might Jake said, "I like who I am. This was all just a mistake. Nathan, I thought I wanted you, but you were a mistake. I don't want you. I don't need you."

Wind started blowing in the room through both the broken window and the door. All the lights in the room came on at once and then went off. Nathan stood at the foot of the bed and spoke very slowly, "It's too late. It's too late."

Margery yelled through the closet door loud and fast. "I love you, Jake. I love you as you are. I love you as my friend. You're like a brother to me. I don't mind your dirty clothes or anything about you. I like you just the way you are. You don't have to change. You certainly don't have to be someone else."

Suddenly there was a sound like a million seagulls screaming. But above the noise Jake's voice boomed out. "I love myself!" This time he meant it. This time he knew it. This time everyone knew it.

Immediately Jake was on his feet and all there. He faced Nathan who was now the one fading fast. "I no longer need you. I never really wanted you. I thought you up and you were a mistake."

Nathan completely disappeared, fading right in front of Jake's eyes.

Margery burst open the closet door and threw her arms around Jake. After several minutes she let go of him, slugged him on the shoulder, and said, "Nice to have you back, chump. Sorry about the window."

Chapter 25

A couple of months later, Margery and Jake were sitting high in a tree talking about how Margery had been asked to join the swim team.

"It's incredible," said Jake. "Simply incredible."

"Aren't I wonderful?" laughed Margery.

"How about me?" said Jake.

"Ya, you haven't done so bad yourself. You're like a new Jake."

"Never," said Jake. "I'm an improved old Jake, thank you."

"Right," said Margery. "Hey, by the way, did you ever find the book?"

"Ya, one day it mysteriously showed up in my sock drawer."

"Something showing up anywhere in your room is hardly mysterious," said Margery.

"Well, maybe," said Jake, "but it was weird it was in my sock drawer."

"If you say so," said Margery.

"Nathan had it checked out," said Jake.

"Ya, I know. I was the one that told you."

Jake continued. "And although you and I seem to be the only ones who even remember he existed, I figured I'd better take it back. So I did."

"That means someone probably has it out right now. Boy, are they in for a surprise," said Margery.

"I just hope they are careful," said Jake.

"What did your dad ever do with all the railings he put around the house?"

"Well, he was so glad he wasn't dizzy anymore he was going to burn them in the fireplace, but my mother gave them to Maria's ballet school."

"Nobody is dizzy anymore?" asked Margery.

"Sam was and I started to panic, but the doctor said it was caused from an inner ear infection. He was underwater too long."

"So who was Nathan?" asked Margery. "Where did he come from?"

"I don't know," said Jake. "I keep wondering if I really thought him up."

"Explain it some other way," said Margery.

"I don't know. I just can't believe that it was — he was real and it was all my fault."

"Well, what was he?" asked Margery. "If you didn't think him up where is he now?"

Right then a cloud went in front of the sun and a huge gust of wind hit their tree, almost knocking them off their branch.

Jake yelled, "Thoughts are real Margery. And I'm so glad I like myself."

The wind stopped and the sun came out.

"Me, too," said Margery.

About the Author

DEAN MARNEY'S grandmother used to refer to him as "the crazy one." He went to school forever and hated every minute of it. Right now, he's a library administrator in Wenatchee, Washington. He lives in Malaga, Washington, on Mud Lake, with his family.

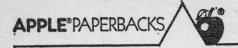